the BAD GUYS

in

THE BADDEST
DAY EVER

TEXT AND ILLUSTRATIONS COPYRIGHT © 2019 BY AARON BLABEY

ALL RIGHTS RESERVED. PUBLISHED BY SCHOLASTIC INC., PUBLISHERS SINCE 1920. 557 BROADWAY, NEW YORK, NY 10012. SCHOLASTIC AND ASSOCIATED LOGOS ARE TRADEMARKS AND/OR REGISTERED TRADEMARKS OF SCHOLASTIC INC. THIS EDITION PUBLISHED UNDER LICENSE FROM SCHOLASTIC AUSTRALIA PTY LIMITED. FIRST PUBLISHED BY SCHOLASTIC AUSTRALIA PTY LIMITED IN 2019.

THE PUBLISHER DOES NOT HAVE ANY CONTROL OVER AND DOES NOT ASSUME ANY RESPONSIBILITY FOR AUTHOR OR THIRD-PARTY WEBSITES OR THEIR CONTENT.

ISBN 978-1-338-30584-5

10 9 8 7 6 5 4 3 2 1   20 21 22 23 24

PRINTED IN THE U.S.A.   23
FIRST U.S. PRINTING 2020

AARON BLABEY

the BAD GUYS

in

THE BADDEST DAY EVER

SCHOLASTIC INC.

That's lovely.

You know . . . I thought you didn't like him.

Are you serious?
He was the snake of my dreams.

Hang in there,
Agent Doom.

I am *so* misunderstood.

Aha!
MR. WOLF?

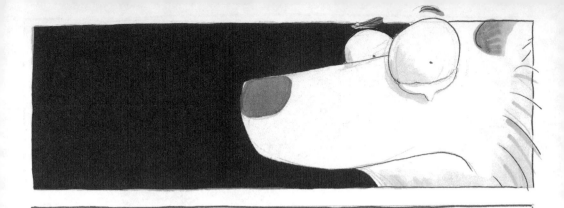

Howdy doody!

TIFFANY FLUFFIT, Channel 6 News. I'm a HUGE fan and I was wondering if you'd be prepared to give me an **EXCLUSIVE INTERVIEW** about the **"TRAGIC DEMISE OF MR. SNAKE"?**

Whaddya say?

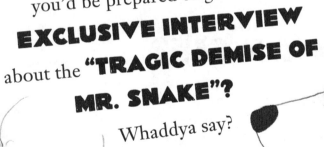

I can think of a few things
I'd like to say to you. But not
right now. You know why?

We're a bit busy at the moment.

· CHAPTER 1 ·
MARMALADE THE CONQUEROR

THERE IS A **BRIGHT** NEW DAWN AND I—
PRINCE MARMALADE
—AM THE SUN!
FROM THIS DAY **FORTH** YOU SHALL
ORBIT MY **TOTAL HOTNESS**
AND GIVE **ETERNAL THANKS** THAT
I SPARED YOUR **WRETCHED**
SOULS.

YOU ARE MINE. FOR NOW AND FOREVER.

YOU'RE WELCOME. SERIOUSLY, DON'T MENTION IT.

SADLY, THE NAME OF MY PLANET CANNOT BE PRONOUNCED BY EARTHLINGS, BUT NEVERTHELESS YOU SHALL LOOK UPON IT WITH WONDER AND AWE . . .

YES!
I AM KDJFLOERHGCOINWERUHCGLEIRWFHEKLWJFHXALHW,
CROWN PRINCE OF THE PLANET :(,
AND BEFORE ME YOU SHALL **KNEEL FOR ALL ETERNITY!**

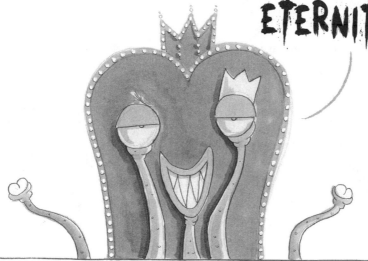

HAHAHAHA!

SORRY, IT'S HARD TO SAY THIS NAME WITH A STRAIGHT FACE ...

REMEMBER THE SAD TALE OF

THE GOOD GUYS CLUB!

WHAT A BUNCH OF LOSERS THEY TURNED OUT TO BE! AND THAT **NAME?** WHAT IDIOT THOUGHT THAT UP?!

HAHAHA!

Don't listen to him.

It is a stupid name.

No, it's not.

That's very nice of you to say, but it is.

And because of it, Mr. Snake is gone.

I hate that stupid name.

DON'T YOU DARE!

I have dedicated **MY LIFE** to the
INTERNATIONAL LEAGUE OF HEROES.
With these ladies right here,
I have fought so many battles and kept
the world safe for so long that I can
barely remember anything else.

Right, girls?

Uh-huh.

I would *die* for the League of Heroes. Without hesitation. But know this—

I would be *proud* to be a member of the **GOOD GUYS CLUB.**

You would?!

The name doesn't matter. It's what you *do* that matters. And what you've all done is amazing. **I'D JOIN YOUR GANG ANY DAY.**

Me too, sugar.

Look, I can see where this is going, but I do have a real issue with the name. It's tragic.

Hear! Hear!

Then why don't we start a new organization?

All of us. Together.

With a *cooler* name.

Like what?

High fives all around, *chicos*!

Awww, Isn't that cute!

It's really convenient, too— STAY RIGHT THERE! It'll make it so much easier to ANNIHILATE you!

YOU WILL NEVER DEFEAT US!

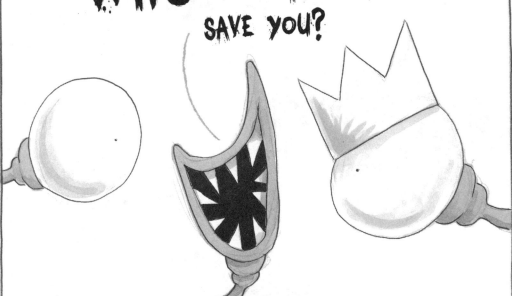

· CHAPTER 2 ·
LEGS, THAT'S WHO

I need to get control of this ship.

And that's just what I'll do.

Rhonda?

SMACK!

SCUTTLE!
SCUTTLE!
SCUTTLE!

I hope you can hear me!
Rhonda can buy me some time, but we're

MASSIVELY OUTNUMBERED.

We need your help.
Please, guys! Get up here!

WE NEED YOU!

This is our chance!

· CHAPTER 3 ·
FROM BOLIVIA, WITH LOVE

Hey, *chico*?

Yeah?

Be careful.

ZOOOM!

So, now what?

Well, sure—we're **OUTNUMBERED.** And no—you guys don't really have an **A GAME** you can bring to this party. But you know what? **WE'VE GOT EACH OTHER'S BACKS.** And that's enough for me.

Plus, we've got ourselves a **REAL LIVE DINOSAUR.** That's something!

And I'm still really good at disguises. I'll just have to do it **"OLD SCHOOL"** without the superpowers.

I do wish we had our superpowers, though, *chico*.

Pepe, who needs superpowers when you have **FAMILY?**

Papa?!

What are you doing
here, Papa?!

Your big brothers and cousins and I
thought you might like some help,

LITTLE PEPE.

Aaaah, they call me

MR. PIRANHA

around here, Papa . . .

HAHAHAHAHA!

That's very good,
Little Pepe.
You've still got it.

Now, *chico*!
Let's have ourselves
an old-fashioned
**BUTT-KICKING
PARTY!**
Whaddya say?!

· CHAPTER 4 ·
GETTING TO KNOW YOU

FLING!

SPLAT!

SPLAT!

SPLAT!

It's Ellen.

Oh. Heh.
Er . . . hi . . .
Ellen.

And who
might you be,
"Mr. Wolf"?

No one's ever asked
me that before . . .

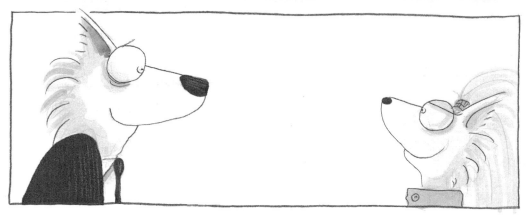

I'm Moe.

Well, Moe . . .

I'll help Rhonda. You help Legs.

Meet you back here.

Legs?!

Are you OK?!

Yep.
It's only
a heart
attack . . .

I'm SO EXCITED you're here,
WOLFIE! Look! It's the

CONTROLS TO
THE SHIP!

So, the only question is . . .

Where do you want me to take her, **CAPTAIN?**

ZAP!

· CHAPTER 5 ·
SHADOW SQUAD G IS A GO!

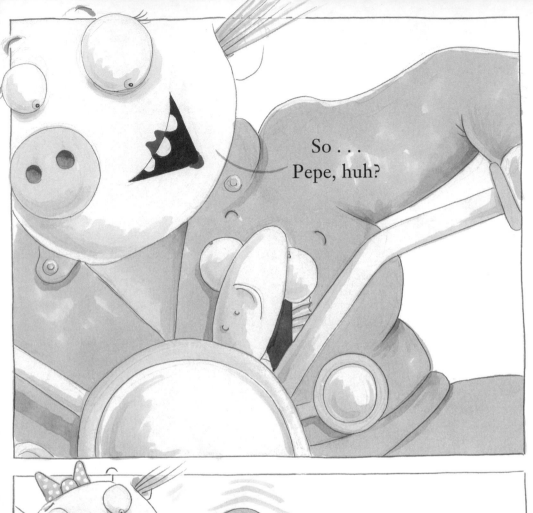

Cute.

I'm
EMMYLOU,
in case you were
wondering.

And look at your
DADDY!

Aliens!
Say hello . . .

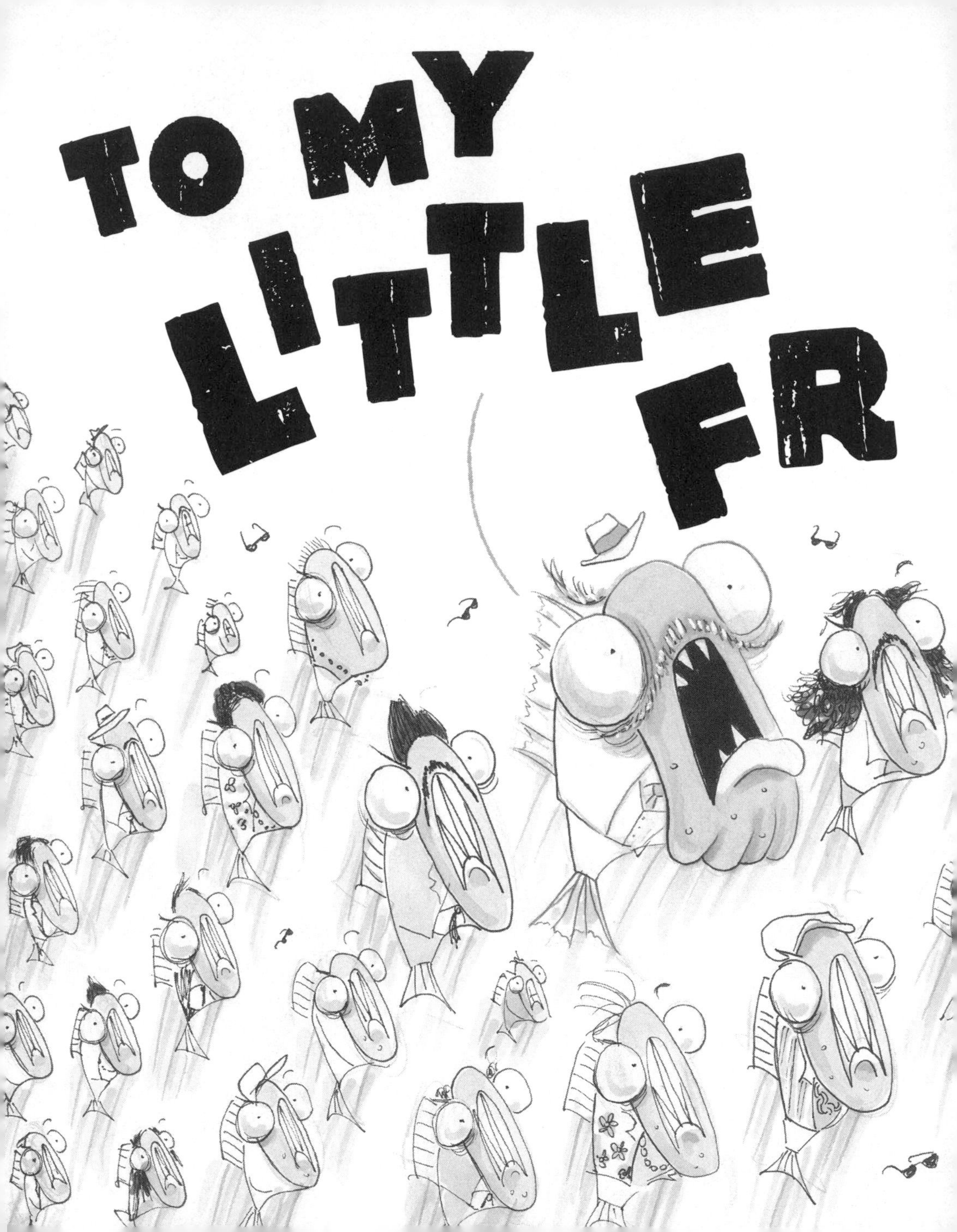
TO MY
LITTLE
FR

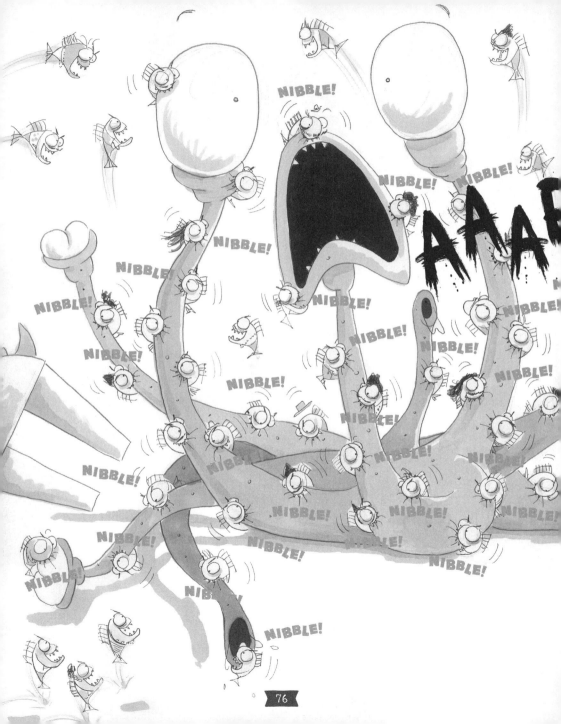

You know, when I first saw that disguise, I had my doubts . . .

PECK!

PECK!

But man, I was *wrong*.

You know it, lady.

I think we might
just have a chance,
Pam, baby!

You go, girlfriend.

· CHAPTER 6 ·
THE ROYAL LUNCHEON

THE AGE OF ME!

Ellen!

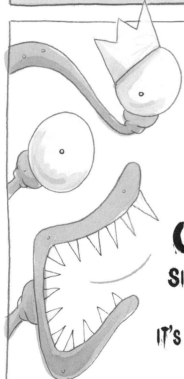

CITIZENS OF EARTH!
SIT BACK, RELAX, AND ENJOY THIS
GLOBALLY TELEVIZED EVENT—
IT'S TIME TO WATCH YOUR MASTER...

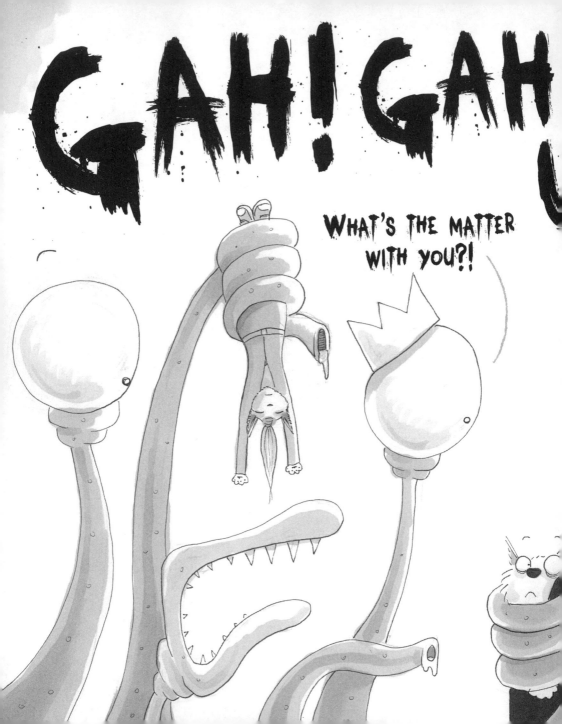

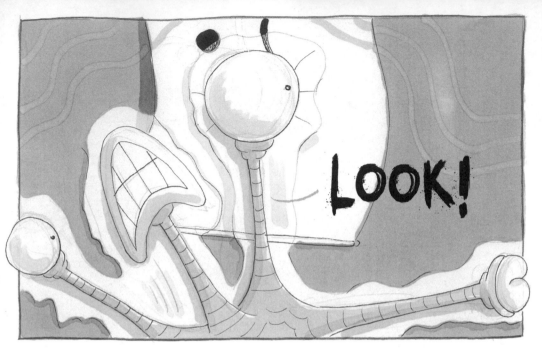

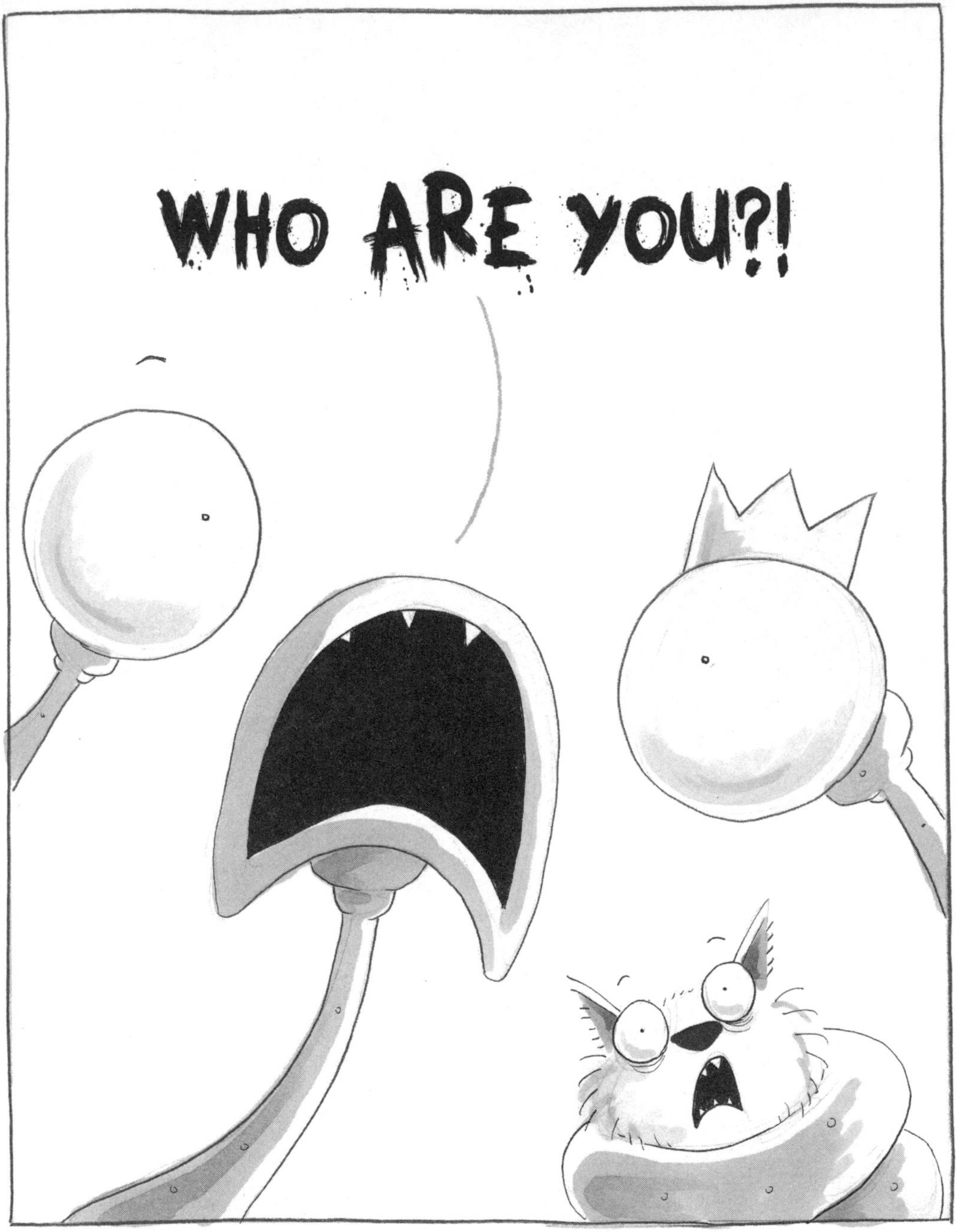
WHO ARE YOU?!

PUT ME

THUD!

THUD!

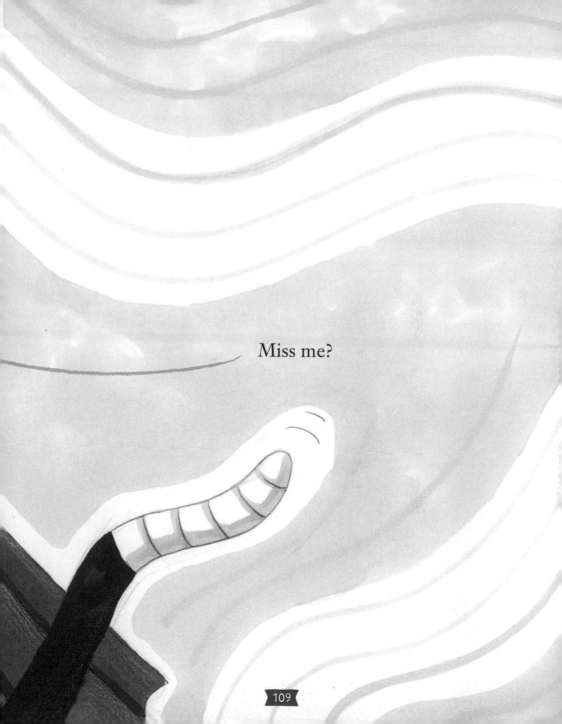

Miss me?

· CHAPTER 7 ·
RETURN OF THE BAD GUY

GUARDS! STOP HIM— NOW!

That's better.

Is that . . . ?

So . . .

You probably have a few questions.

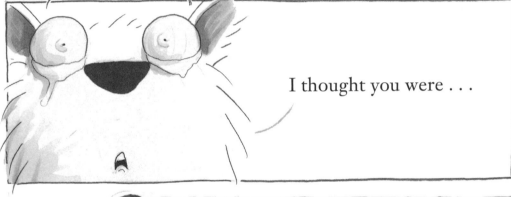

I thought you were . . .

A goner?

I fell into the
mother ship's cannon . . .

just as the aliens started to
drain your superpowers.

And as they sucked in all
your powers . . .

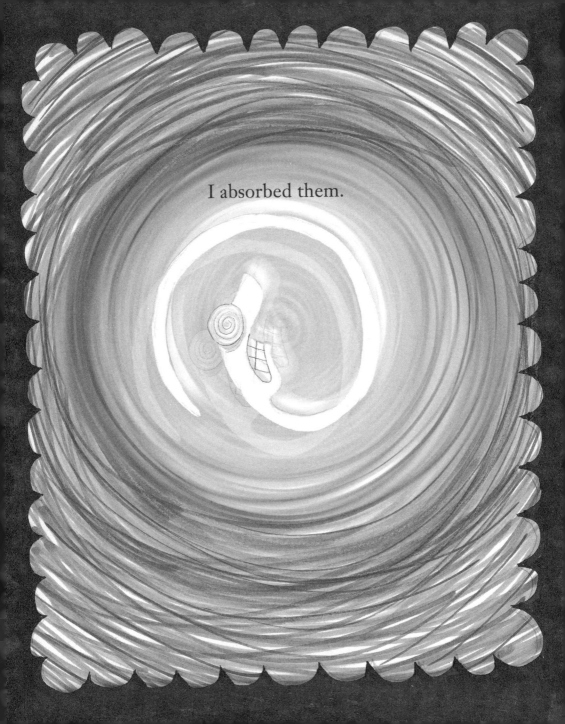

I absorbed them.

All of them.

But then it hit me . . .

I'm speaking now to all the
ALIEN INVADERS!

We've been treating **YOU** the way others have been treating *us* our whole lives.

We decided that because **ONE** of you is a villain, you **ALL** must be.

We *assumed* you were

ALL
DIRTY ROTTEN
BAD GUYS.

And then I heard it . . .

Prince Marmalade.

PRINCE.

And that got
me thinking . . .

Maybe the rest of you were being **FORCED** to behave like this. Maybe you never had a choice.

Maybe you're not all the same. Maybe we're just dealing with

ONE ROTTEN APPLE.

But I'm *hoping* . . .
you'll just decide to
GET
YOURSELVES
FREE.

It's up to you, but . . .

Well, thank you.
Thank you *very much*.

Now . . .

here's the big question . . .

· CHAPTER 8 ·

THE SAD TALE OF KDJFLOER ETC.....

Hermano!
You're here! You're
here! You're here!

We can't believe
you're here!

Yeah, he's here. Geez.
Get *over* it.

I like your T-shirt.

And Rhonda.

Stevie and Rhonda!
We make such a great team!

PAT!
PAT!
PAT!

I'M **NATHAN.**
MARMALADE'S HEAD OF SECURITY.

You don't have to use a fake Earth name anymore. What's your real

ALIEN NAME?

IT'S NATHAN.

I JUST WANTED TO APOLOGIZE AND TRY TO EXPLAIN A LITTLE BIT ABOUT WHAT'S BEEN GOING DOWN . . .

YOU SEE, ON **OUR PLANET**, WE ALL LIVE FOR THOUSANDS OF YEARS. AND EVEN THOUGH PRINCE MARMALADE IS **900** YEARS OLD, TO US HE'S STILL **A KID.** I MEAN, HE HAS THE EMOTIONAL MATURITY OF A **PRESCHOOLER.**

I'M **NOT** KIDDING. HE **LITERALLY** GOES TO PRESCHOOL.

HAPPY-TIME PRESCHOOL

BUT HIS DAD, THE KING OF :(, IS 10,000 YEARS OLD AND HE WAS, LIKE, TOTALLY DISAPPOINTED IN MARMALADE BECAUSE HE'S SO CUTE AND CUDDLY, WHICH IS NOT COOL ON OUR PLANET. YOU KNOW WHAT I'M SAYING?

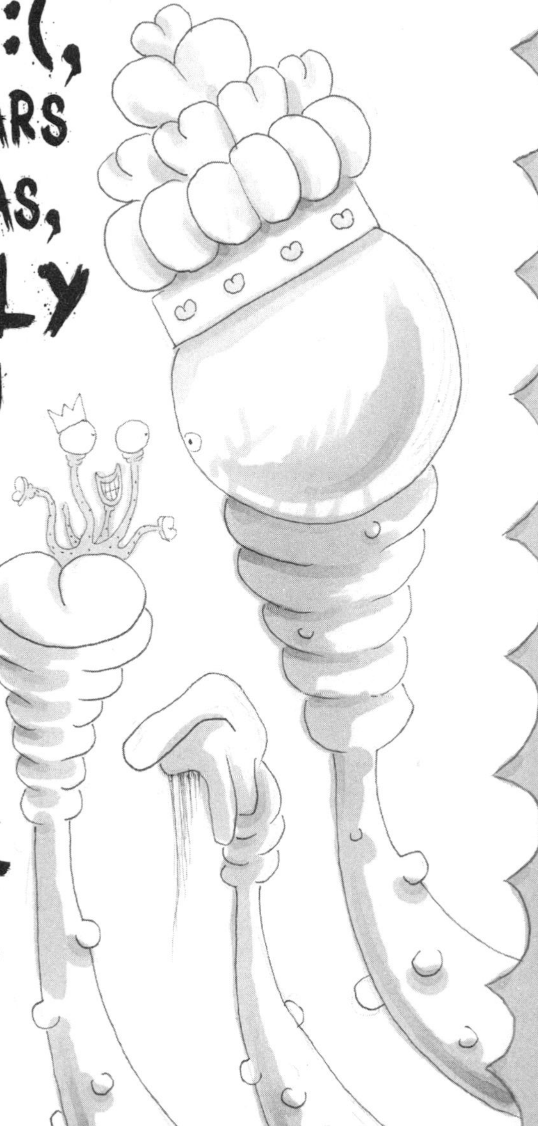

SO ANYWAY, THE KING SENT
MARMALADE OUT INTO THE GALAXY
TO TOUGHEN UP A LITTLE—
TO PROVE THAT HE HAS WHAT IT TAKES TO
BE THE KING ONE DAY.

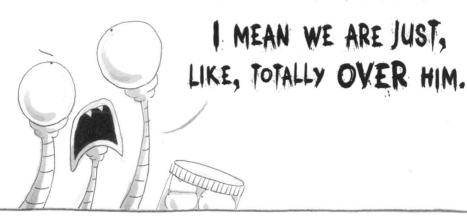

AND HE SENT US WITH MARMALADE, TO MAKE SURE HE WAS OK. BUT HE IS **SUCH** A LITTLE **BULLY.** HE WAS LIKE **"CONQUER THIS!"** AND **"ANNIHILATE THAT!"**

I MEAN WE ARE JUST, LIKE, TOTALLY **OVER** HIM.

SO, YOU KNOW... **THANKS.** AND WE PROMISE TO TAKE HIM TO SOME OTHER GALAXY. **FAR, FAR AWAY.** SO... HOPEFULLY... NO HARD FEELINGS?

COOLIO . . .

Hey, there is one thing . . .

ANYTHING!

GRUUUAAARRG!

I'm not sure if you can do anything about it . . .

but our friend just isn't quite himself . . .

· CHAPTER 9 ·
A VERY GOOD DAY

Here's the moment you've all been waiting for, and . . .

YES!

Here they are—
with a *brand-new name*!
I give you . . .

Wow, what a name!

You can practically see the logo!

YOU GUYS ROCK!

Oh, aren't I the giddy goat . . .

Apologies, everyone!

These suits were NOT designed with six-inch retractable claws in mind. I'm afraid I've shredded a couple putting them on . . .

It's good to have you back, Mr. Snake.

It's good to be back,
Mr. Wolf.

Time to take a bow . . .

LOVE YOU!

Not bad at all.

THE

. . . OR

IS IT?

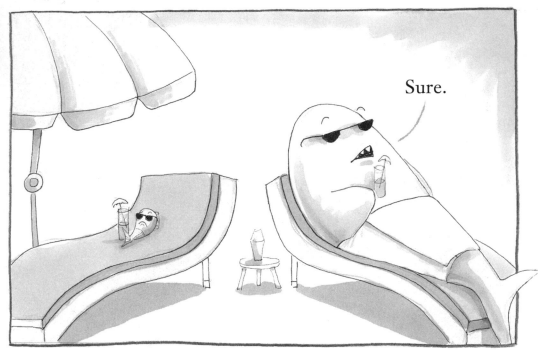

Does it worry you that Mr. Snake is suddenly *so* powerful . . .

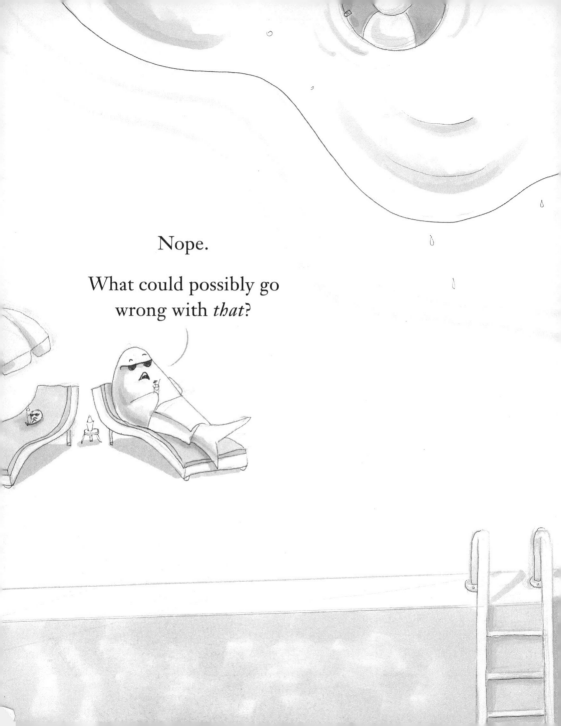

Nope.

What could possibly go
wrong with *that*?

**THE BAD GUYS
WILL BE BACK.**